J F Christopher, Matt F687do
Christopher, Matt.
Football double threat

WITHDRAWN

# FOOTBALL
# DOUBLE THREAT

# FOOTBALL
# DOUBLE THREAT

## Text by Stephanie Peters

LITTLE, BROWN AND COMPANY
Books for Young Readers
New York   Boston

Little, Brown and Company

Hachette Book Group USA
237 Park Avenue, New York, NY 10017
Visit our Web site at www.lb-kids.com

www.mattchristopher.com

First Edition: September 2008

The characters and events portrayed in this book are fictitious.
Any similarity to real persons, living or dead, is coincidental and
not intended by the author.

Library of Congress Cataloging-in-Publication Data

Peters, Stephanie True, 1965–
   Football double threat / [Matt Christopher] ; text written by
Stephanie True Peters. — 1st ed.
      p. cm.
   At head of title:  Matt Christopher the #1 sports series for kids.
   Summary: Feeling guilty after accidentally breaking his friend's leg,
Rocky Fletcher takes on extra duties at school, from selling chocolate
bars and managing his injured friend's student council campaign to
playing both offense and defense on the football team.
   ISBN 978-0-316-01632-2
[1. Football — Fiction.   2. Friendship — Fiction.   3. Guilt — Fiction.
4. Schools — Fiction.]   I. Christopher, Matt.   II. Title.
   PZ7.P441833Fo 2008
   [Fic] — dc22                                            2008010591

10 9 8 7 6 5 4 3 2 1

COM-MO

Printed in the United States of America

Text written by Stephanie True Peters

# FOOTBALL
# DOUBLE THREAT

# 1

Rocky Fletcher entered the middle-school locker room with his duffel bag slung over his shoulder. The twelve-year-old wide receiver greeted a few of his teammates and then headed to an empty row to get into his uniform.

He unzipped the main compartment of his bag and took out his protective gear. First came the shining gold helmet with its image of a hissing, coiled snake on each side — the logo of the Park City Pythons, Rocky's team. Rocky loved that logo. The snake made him think about squeezing the ball tight after making a catch and slithering past the defense into the end zone.

He polished the helmet with his sleeve before putting it on the bench. He reached back into the bag and pulled out his other gear. There were pads to protect his stomach and hips, shoulders and arms, thighs, knees, and shins. His cleats and mouth guard came out next, followed by his team jersey — #83 — and pants. Finally, he pulled out a handheld music player with attached earbuds.

Putting the player aside, Rocky quickly suited up in his pads, pants, jersey, and cleats. A glance at the clock told him there were five minutes to spare — plenty of time to listen to his favorite new song.

He grabbed his music player, put the buds in his ears, and sat on the bench. He thumbed his way around the dial to a playlist he'd named Pre-Game Pump. Then he scrolled down to the song he wanted to hear, tapped a button to start the music, and closed his eyes.

2

A staccato drumbeat filled his ears. It was slow at first but then picked up speed. Rocky tapped his toes along with the rhythm. When a bass guitar joined the drums, his heart seemed to pulse in time with the thrumming tones. Suddenly, an electric guitar wailed out a single, ear-splitting chord. Even though he'd known it was coming, that note sent a rush of adrenaline through Rocky's veins. Heart racing, he drummed his fingers against his thigh pads.

*Wait for it, wait for it,* he thought. *And . . . and . . . NOW!*

As that last word flashed across his brain, the lead singer belted out the first phrases of the song — and Rocky just couldn't sit any longer. He leaped to his feet, punched the air, and bobbed his head to the beat. He would have sung along, but experience had taught him that people who sang to music only they could hear looked foolish. So he settled for mouthing the words and performing a mean air guitar solo.

Suddenly, an arm circled his neck and pulled him into a choke hold. Startled, Rocky broke free and spun around. The arm belonged to his best friend and teammate, Bobby Richards. Standing behind Bobby were five other Pythons. All were clapping and laughing.

Beet red with embarrassment, Rocky hit PAUSE and took out the earbuds.

"Encore! Encore!" Bobby cried then.

"Yeah, yeah, very funny," Rocky muttered. "Don't you guys have something better to do — like get ready for the game?"

Still laughing, everyone except Bobby left to put on the rest of their gear.

"Yo, Rock Star," Bobby said, a wide grin splitting his face. "What were you listening to?"

"That new song from the Phantasms," Rocky replied. "It totally psyches me up, especially the ending. In fact, I want to hear that part before the game." He started to put the buds back in his ears.

Bobby stopped him. "I haven't heard that song yet! Lemme listen, okay?" He made a grab for the player.

Rocky blocked him with his body. "Not a chance!"

"Why not?"

"I bought this player with money I earned mowing lawns this summer. I've only had it a week and I'm not about to loan it out, okay?" Rocky knew he sounded selfish, but he didn't care. He'd worked hard for his player; what if he let Bobby use it and Bobby broke it?

"Fine." Bobby turned away with a grumpy look. But as Rocky started to put the buds in his ears, Bobby whirled back and lunged for the player.

"Bobby! Cut it out! Come on, get back!"

As the two boys tussled for control, Jeff Abbot, the Pythons quarterback, walked by.

"Save it for the game, will you?" he said. "Coach Royson and Coach Ward want us on the field right now!"

5

Rocky and Bobby stopped horsing around immediately. While Rocky stowed the player in his locker, Bobby grabbed their helmets. He tossed Rocky his and then together they ran out of the locker room and toward the gridiron.

"Seriously, Rocky," Bobby said as they jogged onto the field, "I'm dying to hear that song."

"Seriously, Bobby," Rocky replied, "get your own player and you can!"

## 2

The two boys lined up on the field along with their teammates for the pre-game warm-ups.

"Ready, Pythons?" Coach Royson called. "Jumping jacks! Begin!"

The players moved in unison, swinging their arms over their heads and down to their sides, opening and closing their legs, and giving out a loud grunt each time they'd finished a set of ten jacks. Five sets later, they ran in place, lifting their knees as high as possible. Then they did a quick-feet/push-up combo — five seconds of rapid footfalls followed by a drop to the ground

7

for two push-ups. After a series of leg stretches, they followed Mr. Ward, the assistant coach and head of the defensive squad, in a lap around the field.

"Let's hear it!" Coach Ward called. "Py-*thons*! Py-*thons*!"

The team picked up the chant. When they passed the bleachers, Pythons fans joined in. Rocky grinned. That chant did just as much to get his blood pumping as the run and his favorite song had done.

Rocky was breathing hard when he finished the lap. Sweat pricked his hairline. It was a warm afternoon by September standards, but he didn't mind. The heat made his muscles feel loose, and, as for the sweat, heck, what was the point of playing sports if you didn't need to shower after a game?

He paced up and down the sideline. As he did, he passed the Pythons' newest member, a wiry boy named Jared. Unlike the other players, who were gathered in small groups and talking in loud, excited voices, Jared was sitting alone and silent on the bench.

Rocky didn't know much about Jared other than that he'd played soccer for a few years before switching to football this season. Now he was the Pythons kicker, a position he seemed well suited for.

*But not really interested in,* Rocky couldn't help thinking as he eyed the other boy's slack posture and stony expression. *Wonder why he even joined the team?*

*Fweet!* A sharp blast from the official's whistle sent all thoughts other than football from Rocky's mind. It was game time at last!

The Pythons were playing the Shooting Stars, a tough but not impossible-to-beat team. The Pythons won the coin toss and elected to receive first.

Rocky was a wide receiver, but he was also on the kickoff return team. He hurried onto the field with the other members of the special squad. The official placed the ball in the tee, jogged backward out of the way, and blew his whistle again.

The Stars raced forward. Their kicker's right toe connected with the ball, sending it sailing end over end toward the waiting Pythons.

Rocky was in the best position to make the catch. He looked the ball all the way into his hands, tucked it securely against his side, and began to run. He crossed the Pythons forty-yard line . . . the forty-five . . . the fifty . . . and had almost reached the Stars forty-five when *wham!* he was pancaked by a hulking boy in silver and blue.

Coach Royson clapped and nodded with satisfaction. "Good run!" he called as the Pythons offense took to the field.

Rocky stayed on the field. He was breathing hard and smiling when he joined the huddle. Jeff gave him a pat on the back. "You got us good and close, Rocky," he said. "Let's see what else you can do. Bootleg, with a fake handoff to Rasheed and a short pass to Rocky. Got it?"

Rocky and the others nodded their understanding.

Jeff clapped once and called, "Break!"

*Time to make it happen!* Rocky thought.

**3**

**R**ocky's heart was hammering in his chest as he hurried to his spot on the far left of the field. He rubbed his hands on his pants to dry off the sweat. He didn't want to blow the catch because of slippery palms!

The Pythons linemen crouched at the line of scrimmage. Jeff got behind center Joe Dever. Running backs Lars Nielsen and Rasheed Tiwari stood behind and on either side of Jeff. Isaac Brown, who played wide receiver like Rocky, set up on the right.

When everyone was in place, Jeff called the play. Joe snapped the ball between his legs. The moment the ball hit Jeff's waiting hands, both teams exploded into motion.

*Whump! Thud!* "Oof!"

Helmets and pads clashed as the offense collided with the defense in a ferocious head-to-head battle for turf. The Pythons line held steady, giving Jeff time to fade back into the pocket and look for Lars. Lars raced to meet him for the fake.

Rocky, meanwhile, streaked down the left side of the field with the Stars cornerback rushing to cover him.

Now came the bootleg. Jeff spun away from the Stars defense and pretended to give Lars the ball. Lars cradled his empty arms against his stomach and ran as if he had the ball.

As one, the Stars moved to tackle Lars. The fake had worked!

Rocky put on a burst of speed and got clear of his defender. Jeff finished his spin and threw a bullet of a pass. Rocky stretched out his arms, keeping his eyes on the spiraling ball as it shot toward him — and into his waiting hands!

He gathered the ball in close but didn't gain any more ground because the cornerback flattened him. The play was over, but the completed pass had earned the Pythons seven yards. They poked a hole in the Stars defensive line on the next play for first down at the Stars thirty-six-yard line.

"Coach is calling for a running play up the middle," Jeff relayed in the huddle. "Line up in I-formation. Lars, you block for Rasheed. Rasheed, find the hole and run with it. Ready? Break!"

The I-formation found Lars stacked behind Jeff, and Rasheed behind Lars. After the ball was snapped, Lars dashed past Jeff to clear a path for Rasheed's run. Rasheed sprinted toward Jeff. He held one arm across his chest, the other across his stomach, making a perfect target for Jeff to hit with a handoff.

Unfortunately, the handoff never came because Joe slipped and fell after the snap. A defender jumped through the sudden opening, lunged at Jeff, and pulled him to the ground before Jeff could get rid of the ball. It was a loss of three yards, second down and thirteen.

Back in the huddle, Joe started to apologize. Jeff cut him short with a wave. "Forget it. It's over and done. Moving on. Same play, but different results, okay? Break!"

This time, the handoff was successful. Rasheed, one of their biggest, strongest players, rushed for a gain of four yards before being pulled to the ground. He was grinning widely when he joined the huddle.

"Took two of them to bring me down, did you see?" he bragged.

Jeff thumped him on the back and then outlined the next play. "We need to pick up at least six yards. Coach wants more, though, so we're going with the long bomb. Rocky, Isaac, you slant to the center and then back

15

out to the corners. I'll hit whichever of you is open. Right? Break!"

Rocky trotted to his spot. If successful, this play could end in a touchdown. He licked his lips in anticipation. He wanted to be the one to carry the ball into the end zone so badly, he could practically taste it!

Jeff called out the signals. Joe snapped. Ball in hand, Jeff danced back. Rocky and Isaac ran on diagonals toward the center and then darted back to the sidelines.

"Quick feet, quick feet," Rocky urged himself. He had the advantage over his defender. He looked back just as Jeff threw the bomb.

The ball flew toward Rocky, a brown egg spiraling against the deep blue sky. Both Rocky and the Stars cornerback saw it coming. As the ball descended, the cornerback jumped for the interception. But the ball was just out of his reach; it landed in Rocky's reaching hands instead.

Rocky pulled it close, put his head down, and barreled the final yards over the line.

*Fweet!* The officials raised their arms straight up in the air. Touchdown!

Rocky spiked the ball into the turf and gave a whoop. His teammates whooped, too. The Pythons were first on the scoreboard!

**4**

The Pythons didn't celebrate their first touchdown for long. They had to get ready for the extra-point attempt.

Rocky saw Jared stand up in case the coach wanted to try for a one-point kick. But Coach Royson decided to go with a running play for a possible two points instead. Jared sat back down and kicked at the dirt with his cleats.

The Pythons got the two points. Rocky passed Jared as the kicker headed onto the field for the kickoff. Rocky thought about wishing him good luck, but since Jared didn't even glance at him, he changed his mind.

Jared sent the ball through the air into the hands of the Shooting Stars and then it was time for the defense to take to the field.

"It's freeze time!" Bobby called as he headed onto the field. "We're going to stop 'em cold!"

Bobby played safety for the Pythons. He and the rest of the defense did their jobs well and kept the Stars from scoring that possession.

But the Stars defense was just as strong. In fact, the Stars and the Pythons traded the ball back and forth throughout the rest of the quarter without either team scoring. Then, early in the second quarter, the Stars tied it all up with a touchdown and a two-point conversion. The score stayed knotted until just before halftime, when the Pythons pushed into the end zone for six more points. Their two-point attempt failed, however, and the two teams left the field with the scoreboard reading Pythons 14, Shooting Stars 8.

During the break, Coach Royson praised

his players for their hard work — and then sternly reminded them not to let up for one minute. If they did, he warned them, the Stars had a very good chance to walk away with the victory.

The Pythons took that warning to heart. It was the Stars' turn to receive, but they could do nothing with their possession because the Pythons defense shut them down.

It was a different story when the Pythons got their hands on the ball. They marched steadily down the gridiron into easy scoring range. Isaac caught a short pass from Jeff at the Stars three and leaped over the line into the end zone. Another touchdown, for a total of twenty points!

With a comfortable twelve-point lead, Coach Royson called for Jared to kick the extra-point attempt.

The Pythons kicking team was made up of both offensive and defensive linemen. Their job was to stop the Shooting Stars from rushing Jared. Liam Crimintz, the second string quarterback, was on the field too, acting as ball holder for Jared. Bobby and Rocky, usually on the field at opposite times, now had a rare moment to stand together and watch the play from the sideline.

"Think Jared can send it through the up-rights?" Bobby asked Rocky.

Rocky shrugged. "He's done it before."

Bobby glanced around and then, in a low voice, asked, "Think he'll be psyched if he does? Or will he just go sit down and not say anything, like always?"

Rocky lowered his voice too. "Yeah, what *is* it with him? You think he even *likes* football?"

"I don't know," Bobby replied. "But I guess it doesn't matter, so long as he does what he's here to do."

"Yeah, maybe." But Rocky couldn't help thinking that if he was that miserable play-ing a sport, he'd quit or try something else instead.

They turned their attention back to the field. Liam snared Joe's long snap and placed

21

the ball on end just as Jared came forward to kick it. One solid boot later, the Pythons had another point on their side of the board. Jared stayed on the field for the kickoff and then made his way to the bench.

"Nice kicks, Jared," Coach Royson called.

"Thanks," Jared mumbled as he sat down.

"Yes, well done, son!" Coach Ward echoed warmly.

Jared stiffened and shot Coach Ward a cold look. Rocky saw the coach blink and turn away.

*Okay, that was weird!* Rocky thought. But then the defensive squad jostled past him onto the field and he forgot all about the kicker.

The Shooting Stars failed to reach first down and were forced to punt. The Pythons got the ball back on their own thirty-two. It was midway through the third quarter and the Pythons had a solid thirteen-point lead. That prompted Coach Royson to make a few changes to the lineup. Jeff was replaced by Liam, while a short, chubby boy named Vincent went in for Rocky.

Rocky grabbed a cup of water and sat on the bench to rest and watch the action on the field. Unfortunately, there wasn't much to see there because Liam was off his game. The first time he threw the ball it soared over Isaac's head to bounce incomplete several feet beyond him. The next time, he bobbled a handoff. He had a few good plays after that but then seemed confused about which player was on his team because he threw the ball directly into the arms of a Shooting Stars safety — who turned the interception into a 60-yard run!

Out came the Pythons offense. Liam took off his helmet and slumped on the bench, dismay etched on his face. A few players, including Rocky, offered him halfhearted murmurs of encouragement, but Liam just looked away.

Meanwhile, the Pythons defense was back on the field. They tried to keep the Stars from scoring, but failed. With the score now 21 to 14, the two teams lined up for the extra-point attempt.

"They're going for two!" Coach Royson warned his team.

That's just what happened — or started to, anyway. The Stars center snapped the ball to the quarterback. The quarterback skipped back several steps, pump-faked the ball, and then began to run it in himself. He'd only gone a few steps when Alan Dobbs, one of the Pythons defensive ends, broke free and charged him.

The quarterback never saw the tackle coming. W*ham!* Alan slammed him from the side. The ball squirted from his grasp and shot straight up into the air.

Quick as a wink, Bobby darted forward, nabbed the ball before it hit the ground, and took off!

**5**

The Pythons and their fans roared and cheered as Bobby's cleats ate up the yards. Three Shooting Stars players pounded after him, but Bobby had a few steps' lead. He made it past the Pythons' thirty, their thirty-five, the forty — and had an open field in front of him!

"Go! Go!" Rocky yelled. He jumped up and down, whooping loudly.

The Stars hadn't given up, though. As Bobby approached their twenty, one of them made a desperate lunge for Bobby's feet. Bobby stumbled. For a moment, it looked like he was going to fall. But he righted himself and danced the last yards into the end zone.

*Fweet!* Touchdown!

Then there was another whistle blast. The Stars coach had called for a time-out.

Bobby was breathing hard but grinning from ear to ear when he jogged to the sideline.

"That was awesome!" Rocky cried.

Coach Ward was just as effusive with his praise. "Well done, Bobby! That's the kind of heads-up play that marks the difference between a good player and a great player!"

Rocky saw the coach glance over at Jared as he spoke those words. Jared returned his gaze for a split second before getting up and walking onto the field for the extra-point kick.

*He moves like he has all the time in the world,* Rocky thought, wondering again why Jared was playing for the Pythons when it was so obvious he had no interest in the game.

Bobby's touchdown — and the extra point,

another successful kick by Jared — seemed to take the wind out of the Shooting Stars sails. Their play after the kickoff was sloppy and they quickly lost possession. Their defense was just as lackluster. When the final buzzer sounded, the score was Pythons 28, Stars 14.

The two teams walked through the "good game" hand-slap lines and then went their separate ways. Rocky was happy his team had won, although part of him wished the game had been a little less lopsided at the end. Still, a win was a win — and he wasn't about to complain!

The mood in the locker room was raucous. Boys rehashed the game in loud voices, laughing at other players' mistakes and bragging about their own good plays. Then Joe picked up a water bottle, stood on a bench, and squirted water into the air. Those caught in the sudden cold shower roared with surprise. They turned on Joe, pelting him with sweaty socks and spraying him with water from their own bottles.

The floor turned wet and slippery beneath Rocky's muddy cleats. He sat on the bench to take them off. Suddenly, a loud wail pierced through the laughter — it came from Bobby, who appeared from around the corner. He had taken off his gear and was just in a pair of shorts. He was singing out loud and drumming to a beat. Only *he* knew what the song was, though, because he was listening to it on Rocky's music player!

"Very funny, Bobby," Rocky said. He got off the bench and held out his hand. "Ha, ha. Now give it back!"

Bobby gave Rocky a wicked grin, stuck the player in his waistband, and snapped his fingers in time to the music.

"Hey, come on," Rocky said, louder this time. "Take the player out of there, man! You might damage it — or worse, sweat all over it!"

Bobby danced a circle just out of Rocky's reach. Then he stopped next to bench, turned his back, and began to play air guitar. It was a perfect imitation of Rocky's earlier performance. The other players started laughing.

Rocky flushed a dull red. Then he lunged toward Bobby, intending to pin his arms at his sides and wrestle the player free.

The tackle caught Bobby off balance. His feet slipped on the wet concrete floor and he fell. As he did, his legs slammed against the bench's edge. Rocky fell on top of him.

*Crack!* There was a sound like a dry branch snapping in two. For a split second Rocky thought the sound was his music player breaking. Then he heard someone cry out in pain. The cry came from underneath him — Bobby!

Strong hands lifted Rocky up and off. Bobby dropped to the floor and rolled onto his back, grasping his leg and writhing in agony.

The coaches came running. "Just lay still, son," Coach Royson said, kneeling alongside the whimpering boy. "Let me see what is the matter."

The coach's body was blocking Rocky's view so he couldn't see what was wrong. But when he heard the coach suck in his breath, he guessed it must be bad. Coach Ward's hurried 911 call confirmed his guess.

Twenty minutes later, Bobby was in an ambulance on his way to the emergency room. The other Pythons were slowly and quietly gathering their gear. The coaches were in deep conversation in the office. And Rocky was sitting on the bench — the bench where his best friend had just broken his leg, thanks to him.

There was a strange whispering sound near his feet. He looked around and saw his music player lying on the floor. Music was piping from the earbuds.

Rocky picked up the player and stared at it without really seeing it. Instead, he saw his friend's face, contorted with pain and as pale as snow.

*It's all my fault,* he thought miserably. *If I hadn't been such a selfish jerk, Bobby would be fine.*

He switched off the music. *It's all my fault.*

**6**

**P**ythons, gather around!" Coach Royson and Coach Ward emerged from the office. They looked grim.

"I just got off the phone with Bobby's mother. I'm afraid the news isn't good," Coach Royson reported. "He fractured his femur just above the knee. He's out for the season."

There was a collective groan of dismay. A few players shot Rocky angry looks. He avoided their eyes but couldn't stop the red flush from creeping up his neck to his face.

Then Coach Royson called his name.

"Rocky, I'd like you and Jared to join me and Coach Ward in the office, please."

Rocky swallowed hard and stood to follow the coaches. He wondered if he was going to be chewed out for causing Bobby's accident. But, if so, why was Jared coming along too? Jared hadn't been anywhere near where the other boys were horsing around.

Coach Royson settled into the chair behind his desk. "Grab a seat, boys," he said. "Coach Ward has something he wants to talk to you about. Coach?"

"I know you're both upset about Bobby," Coach Ward said, "and we are too. That being said, we're going to need someone to play safety. I think the two of you might be good candidates."

Rocky's jaw dropped. "Really? Wow, I —"

"Before you give your answer, Rocky," Coach Royson interrupted, "I want you to think long and hard about what it would mean. Being a two-way player — that is, playing both offense and defense — can be very demanding. You'd be doing a great deal of running. And you'd have to bone up on your tackling skills too."

"That would mean extra practice time with me — and with Jared, too, of course," Coach Ward put in. "So if you're not able to commit to that, for whatever reason, you need to let me know now so I can talk to another player."

Rocky's head was spinning. He had thought he was going to be yelled at, not offered the chance to play Bobby's position! Then he thought of something.

"Coach Royson, what about Vincent? He's our sub. Won't he expect to take over for Bobby?"

The coach took off his glasses and rubbed his eyes. "Vincent is moving out of state next week," he said in a tired voice.

"What?" Rocky cried in surprise. "He never said anything about that!"

"He didn't know. His parents only told

him — and Coach Ward and me — last night. In any event, he will not be around to replace Bobby. That's why we're talking to you and Jared."

Rocky had almost forgotten the other boy was there. Jared hadn't said a word throughout the discussion, although Coach Ward had made it sound as if he had already agreed to train for the safety position.

Now Jared spoke up for the first time. "Why me?" He sounded wary.

"You're one of the fastest kids on the team," Coach Royson explained. "And from what I've seen in practice, you have a good instinct for defense. Coach Ward told me you played midfield on your soccer team, right?"

Jared nodded.

"That explains it, then. You had to be fast and able to read the offense to play that position well."

"You had to know how to kick too," Coach Ward put in. "That's why we made you our kicker."

Jared let out an impatient huff. "Kicking a soccer ball is totally different from kicking a football. Everyone knows that."

Rocky squirmed uncomfortably at the disgust in Jared's voice. Coach Royson gave Coach Ward a meaningful glance. Coach Ward's face twitched, but other than that he didn't show any sign of anger. Instead, he spoke lightly and carefully.

"Yes, that's true, Jared. And playing defense in football is different from playing defense in soccer." He leaned forward and fixed his gaze on the boy. "The question is, are you up to learning the position or are you going to back down from the challenge?"

Jared returned the gaze. "I'm not going to back down!" he replied.

"Good." Coach Ward straightened. "Then it's settled. You and Rocky will have extra practices with me to learn the safety position. I'll be in touch with the time."

"Thank you, boys, you may go now," Coach Royson said.

Jared stood up fast, his metal chair scraping against the floor with a loud shriek. Rocky was about to follow him out the door when Coach Royson called him back.

"Rocky, Mrs. Richards asked if you'd deliver Bobby's gear to their house. You can drop it by tomorrow. Bobby should be home from the hospital by then."

The sound of Bobby's bone snapping suddenly echoed in Rocky's memory. He shook his head to clear it out and said, "Sure thing, coach."

"Good. When you do, would you bring him one of these too?" The coach handed him two heavy cardboard boxes. "The other one is for you, of course."

Rocky almost groaned aloud when he saw the boxes. They each contained thirty big chocolate bars. The candy was for the team's fund-raiser; they cost a dollar each and every player was required to sell a boxful to help pay for equipment and league fees. They had three weeks in which to sell them all. Any unsold bars could not be returned. The player had to pay for those himself.

The fund-raiser was one of Rocky's least favorite duties — knocking on the neighbors' doors was only really fun at Halloween. But he had no choice in the matter, especially since after buying his music player, he didn't have thirty dollars. Promising the coach to bring Bobby his candy as well as his gear, he picked up both boxes and left.

# 7

The next afternoon, Rocky loaded Bobby's gear bag onto the back of his bike, stuck the box of candy into his backpack, and rode to Bobby's house. The load on his back seemed light at first, but as he rode, the pack's straps dug deeper and deeper into his shoulders. When he finally reached Bobby's driveway, he took off the pack and rubbed the sore spots with relief.

"You think that hurts," a wan voice said, "you should try having your leg broken."

"Bobby?" Rocky looked around but didn't see his friend. "Where are you?"

"Back here, on the screened-in porch." A hand waved from behind an open window.

Rocky picked up the gear bag and backpack and made his way to the porch. He pushed open the door and stared.

Bobby was sitting in an easy chair with a video game controller in his lap. Next to him was a small table with the television remote, a bowl of chips, and a tall glass of root beer. A pair of crutches lay on the floor. And one of his legs was propped up on an ottoman, a thick white cast extending from the top of his thigh to below his knee.

"Whoa," Rocky breathed. He sat on the floor next to him. "Does it — does it hurt?"

Bobby shrugged but didn't stop playing his game. "Yeah. Especially at night."

"Oh." Rocky didn't know what to say after that. Then he remembered why he'd come. "I brought some stuff for you."

He held out Bobby's gear bag. Bobby glanced at it but didn't reach for it. "Just put it on the floor," he mumbled.

Rocky set the stuff next to the crutches. Then he pulled the box of chocolate bars out of his backpack. "Um, I've got your fundraiser candy here too," he said. "You want me to put that with the other stuff?"

Bobby didn't take his eyes off the television screen. "I guess. Although I doubt I'll get around to selling any of it."

"You have to sell it," Rocky reminded him. "If you don't, you have to buy it yourself. Besides, the coaches won't like it if you don't even try."

Bobby thrust the controller away then. "Big deal. It's not like I'm going to be playing or anything. I'll just be sitting on the sidelines like a lump. If I even bother going to the games."

Rocky's stomach gave a sudden, hard squeeze of guilt. "Bobby, I'm so sorry about your leg," he said in a low voice. "If I had just let you use my music player, you wouldn't be sitting here with that cast."

Bobby toyed with the hem of his T-shirt.

41

He seemed on the verge of saying something but didn't. Then he sighed. "Whatever. It doesn't matter now. I'm out for the season and nothing's going to change that."

"Yeah," Rocky agreed lamely. "It, um, it really stinks."

Bobby shook his head angrily. "You know what stinks the most? The fact that Vincent is taking over my position. I mean, I like the guy and all, but it still kills me to think of him playing my spot."

Rocky gulped. It hadn't occurred to him that Bobby might not have heard about Vincent — or that he might resent the person replacing him on the field.

"Actually, it's not Vincent," he told Bobby. He explained how their teammate was moving.

Bobby stared. "So who are they putting in my position?"

Rocky took a deep breath. "Well, Jared, for one."

"The *kicker*?" Bobby's anger flared into

outrage. "He doesn't even want to be on the team!"

"I know. But he said he'd do it."

Bobby shook his head in disgust and then asked, "So who else?"

"Who else what?"

"You said, 'Jared, for one,'" Bobby reminded him impatiently. "So who else?"

"Oh. Right. Um, promise you won't be mad?"

Bobby narrowed his eyes. "Who *is* it, Rocky?"

"It's me."

Bobby blinked in surprise. Then his expression turned blank. He turned away from Rocky, pushed a button on the controller, and restarted his game.

Rocky stared at his toes, miserable. For more than a minute, the only sounds came from the television.

Then, his eyes on the screen, Bobby asked, "You think you'll be any good at it?"

"Not as good as you," Rocky replied loyally. "You're the best."

43

His answer earned him a twitch of a smile from Bobby. "You got that right."

"I'll probably mess everything up! Totally! And Jared? Forget about him! Like you said, he doesn't even want to be there."

He started telling Bobby about Jared's reactions to Coach Ward's comments, but Bobby cut him off abruptly. "Rocky, listen, my leg's kinda hurting."

Rocky took the hint and stood up. "I gotta go anyway. Got to sell some candy, you know?"

Bobby glanced down at the chocolates for the first time. "That box looks heavy."

"Yeah, it is."

Bobby was quiet for a moment. He seemed to be considering something. Then he cleared his throat and said, "Say, Rock Star, I don't suppose you could . . . oh, never mind."

"Could what?"

"No, no, it's too much to ask." Bobby picked up the controller but didn't start playing. Instead, he looked at the box of candy again. "It's just that . . ."

"Just *what*?"

"Well, I'm not very good on the crutches and, like I said, my leg hurts. I don't know if I can go door-to-door to sell all those chocolate bars. My mom just started a new job so I doubt she can drive me. My dad's on this new health kick so he probably won't want to be near it. And I don't have thirty dollars to pay for them."

Rocky finally got what Bobby was driving at. "You want me to sell your candy for you?"

Bobby looked up hopefully. "Would you?"

Rocky grinned. "Not a problem! It's the least I can do since . . . but first, if your leg can stand my company, let me take a turn at that game. It looks awesome!"

But Bobby held the controller out of reach. "Forget it, man! You've got doorbells to ring! Now get outta here!"

**8**

Rocky spent the next hour and a half biking from one house to another with Bobby's candy. Unfortunately, many people turned him away, saying his teammates had beaten him to the sale. Still, he managed to sell twelve bars — leaving eighteen to go. Eighteen, plus his full box of thirty, he reminded himself, making forty-eight chocolate bars in all.

*Eesh*, he thought as he returned home and put Bobby's half-empty box alongside his full one. *This'll take forever — unless I get some help!*

"Say, Mom," he asked Mrs. Fletcher over dinner later, "wouldn't you like to sell some candy bars at work?"

His mother just laughed. "Gee, honey, since I work for a dentist, that probably wouldn't be a good idea, would it?"

"Oh. I guess not." Rocky turned to his father. "Say, Dad —"

"Sorry, son, but that's a no-go at my office. My co-workers are tired of being pestered to buy stuff from other people's kids." He looked at Rocky's crestfallen face and laughed. "Tell you what, though. I'll buy a couple bars myself, bring them to work, and eat them in the lunchroom. If anyone asks for a sample, I'll tell them where they can get one of their own."

"Thanks, Dad, that'd be great!"

Just then, the phone rang. Rocky answered it.

"Uh, hi, this is Jared," the voice on the other end said. "Coach Ward asked me to call you. He's arranged for us to use the football field tomorrow at three. That good for you?"

Rocky groaned inwardly. School got out at two thirty. Regular practice started at three thirty. He'd planned to use the hour in between to run home and call his grandparents. He was going to ask them to buy — and maybe help him sell — some candy. But he told Jared he'd be at the field and hung up.

"Rocky," his mother called, "if you're done on the phone, please load the dishwasher and then head to your room and finish your homework. Remember, you have to keep your grades up if you want to keep playing football!"

Chores, school, candy, extra football practice — Rocky pressed his thumbs to his eyes. It was going to be one busy fall!

Rocky wasn't certain Bobby was going to be at school the next day. But there he was in class, surrounded by students signing his cast.

The crowd broke up when their teacher, Mrs. Ryan, came into the room and clapped her hands.

"We're starting our unit on geology today," she announced. "Geology is the study of the Earth and what it's made of. This week we'll be learning about the three basic types of rocks: the igneous, the sedimentary, and the metamorphic. Then, tomorrow, I will be taking you on a walking trip to the local park to collect samples for you to study throughout the remainder of the week. Any questions?"

Bobby raised his hand. "Can I collect and study Rocky?" he asked innocently.

When the class had stopped laughing, Mrs. Ryan told them to open their science books to the geology chapter. As they read, Rocky discovered that he was interested in the material. Unlike some of the other sciences, geology made sense to him.

Maybe it's just because my name is Rocky, he joked to himself.

"Before I forget," Mrs. Ryan said at the end of class, "you each need to bring a resealable zipper bag to school tomorrow to put your rock samples in. And wear old clothes because you're going to get dirty!"

**9**

The rest of the school day was uneventful. When the final bell rang at two thirty, Rocky stowed his homework in his backpack and hurried to the gym for practice with Coach Ward. Liam and Lars were there too, getting suited up.

"Hello, Rocky," the coach greeted him warmly. "Glad you could make it. I asked Lars and Liam here to run some plays with you and Jared." He looked around and frowned. "Where is Jared, anyway?"

"I haven't seen him yet, coach," Rocky replied.

Coach Ward pursed his lips but didn't say

anything other than to tell the boys to go to the field and warm up.

They were just finishing a lap when Jared arrived. Coach Ward was right behind him, his expression dark.

"If you're going to be a part of this team," Rocky heard the coach say angrily, "I expect you to follow its rules. That includes being on time."

"I never asked to be part of this team, remember?" Jared flared back. "I'm only here because —"

The other boys drew alongside the pair just then and Jared bit back whatever he was about to say.

Coach Ward slapped his clipboard against his thigh. "All right, all right," he said after a moment of awkward silence. "Let's get started."

He began with a rundown on what a safety did. Rocky, Lars, and Liam already knew, but since it was Jared's first year playing, Rocky figured the coach wanted to be sure the other boy had the same knowledge.

"The two safeties are the last line of defense," Coach Ward explained. "If a ball carrier gets past that line, chances are he'll have a clear run into the end zone."

He flipped over his clipboard to show them a drawing of a typical defensive lineup. He pointed to the free safety in its spot farthest from the line of scrimmage, and the strong safety, who lined up closer to that line and opposite the offense's tight end. In front of the safeties were the three linebackers; the linebackers were flanked by two cornerbacks. The two defensive ends and two defensive tackles were at the line of scrimmage.

"The name of the game in defense is: stop the guy with the ball," the coach continued. "After the snap, the ends and tackles immediately try to break through the offensive line to stop the play from getting off the ground. The linebackers are there to shut down the running plays by tackling the ball carrier. If the linebackers can't stop the ball carrier and the ball carrier runs to the outside, the cornerback on that side of the field stops him. If the run is to the inside or if the cornerback can't get to him, the safeties try for the tackle."

He paused to make sure the boys were following along. They all nodded, even Jared.

"Regardless of whether it's a running play or a pass play, the linemen's and linebackers' jobs don't change much. But cornerbacks and safeties have to be alert for the pass play because it's their job to cover the eligible receivers in order to eliminate them as targets for the quarterback to hit. Cornerbacks usually cover wide receivers. Safeties cover anyone else — tight end, back — who runs down the field for a pass. Questions?"

There were none.

"Okay, then let's try a couple of simple passing drills. Liam, you'll be quarterbacking. I'll snap to you. Lars, you're the receiver. Rocky, you cover Lars. Liam will have a count of five to get off a pass."

"What am I supposed to do?" Jared asked.

"You watch and learn," Coach Ward said shortly. "Offense, come here and I'll outline the play."

Lars and Liam huddled with the coach. Then they clapped their hands and broke for the play. Coach Ward took the ball and crouched with it at the fifty-yard line. Liam bent down behind him, hands ready for the snap. Lars hustled to a spot on their left and got into a three-point stance. Rocky lined up opposite him but back from the line of scrimmage.

Liam barked out the signals. The coach snapped the ball. As Liam faded back and Lars took off, the coach began to count backward from five in a loud voice.

Lars ran straight ahead. Rocky moved to cover him. Lars stutter-stepped and then darted to the outside. Rocky, not fooled, mirrored his every move.

Unfortunately, he was so busy watching Lars that he forgot to watch for the pass. *Thunk!* The ball hit Lars right in the numbers just as the coach yelled, "One!" Lars ran a few steps and then turned back with a wide grin.

"Good coverage, Rocky," Coach Ward called. "But you've got two eyes. One has to be on the quarterback, the other on your man."

Rocky nodded and tried to slow his breathing. Playing safety was harder than he'd expected!

It was Jared's turn next so Rocky moved to the sidelines to watch. Liam and Coach Ward lined up as before. But this time, Lars stood on their right. Jared took his position facing him.

When the ball was snapped, Lars ran right past Jared. Jared backpedaled to keep himself between Lars and Liam. Liam let loose with the pass. The ball spiraled through the air. Lars jumped to make the catch — and Jared shoved him in midair!

*Fweeeet!* The coach's whistle shrieked.

"Pass interference!" he bellowed at Jared. "If you had done that in a game, it would have been an automatic first down for the offense."

Jared stopped in his tracks and scowled. "But you said I was supposed to eliminate the receiver as a target!"

"By covering him, not by decking him," Coach Ward said sarcastically. "You can only tackle the receiver *after* he catches the ball. If it looks like he can catch it, you have to let him. Unless you think you can catch it instead. That's called a —"

"I *know* what it's called," Jared interrupted. "It's an interception." He stormed off to the sidelines muttering, "I'm not an idiot. If you'd *told* me I couldn't hit the guy before the catch, I wouldn't have."

Rocky gave him a sideways glance as he passed him on the field. He suddenly wondered which Jared disliked more, football or Coach Ward — and why he bothered to play for the Pythons if he hated both so much!

**10**

The remaining safety practice sped by. Rocky began to get a feel for keeping his eyes on both receiver and ball, as the coach had instructed. Jared too seemed to improve, although grudgingly. Toward the end, both were able to cover Lars so well that Liam failed to get off passes before the coach finished his countdown.

Their private practice ended when Coach Royson appeared. Moments later, the rest of the Pythons hit the field for warm-ups. Rocky, Lars, Liam, and Jared were given permission to take a quick water break since they were already warmed up.

Rocky took off his helmet, popped open his water, and lifted it to his mouth. Suddenly, someone reached out and tipped the bottle upside down. Water gushed down Rocky's chin and onto his jersey before he could wrench the bottle free. He spun around, sputtering, to find Bobby standing there.

"Gotcha!" Bobby said.

"What did you do that for?" Rocky grumbled.

Bobby grinned. "You were looking so hot playing my position, I thought I better do something to cool you off."

"Thanks for nothing," Rocky said.

"So how's it going out there?" Bobby asked. "How's the new kid doing?"

"All right, I guess," Rocky replied. "You got any pointers you want to pass along, though?"

"Actually, Rock Star," Bobby said, "I'm here because I have something important to ask you."

"If it's about your chocolate bars, I'm

working on it!" The words came out more sharply than he had intended. Out of the corner of his eye, he saw Jared glance at them with curiosity.

"No, it's not about the chocolate, but thanks again for taking care of that for me. My leg" — Bobby grimaced then, moved both crutches to beneath one arm, and sank slowly onto the bench — "still isn't feeling that great." He held up a hand. "But don't you worry about that, buddy, I'm sure it'll stop aching . . . eventually."

Rocky's anger melted into guilt. "So what did you want to ask me, anyway?"

"I have to tell you something first." Bobby puffed out his chest. "I am going to run for student council!"

"No kidding!" Rocky remembered seeing the signs around the middle school announcing the upcoming elections for the student-run government. But he had no idea Bobby was interested in entering the race. In fact, he recalled that last year,

Bobby had made fun of the people running, calling them blowhards and teachers' pets.

"That's not all!" Bobby pointed a finger at Rocky. "I want you to be my campaign manager!"

Rocky blinked. "Your . . . what?"

"Campaign manager! You know, the guy who helps get me elected. You think up slogans, hang posters, talk me up around school, that kind of thing."

"I don't know, Bobby. It sounds like a lot of work and now that I've got these extra football practices . . ." His voice trailed off uncertainly.

Bobby's smile vanished. When he spoke, he sounded hurt. "Oh. Right. Extra practices."

He let out a long, dejected sigh. "Maybe running for student council is a dumb idea, anyway. It's just that I've got all this free time, you know, what with my leg in a cast and everything. If only you hadn't tackled me . . ."

His words hung in the air between them. Rocky broke the silence.

"Is that all I'd have to do?" he asked. "Think up slogans and hang posters?"

Bobby brightened instantly. "Yeah, that's it! I think so, anyway. Actually, I'm not really sure. I wanted to know if you'd be my manager before I checked into the whole thing, you know? So will you?"

"I — sure, Bobby, I'll be your manager."

"Awesome! There's a meeting for all candidates Wednesday at two thirty."

"Okay," Rocky agreed reluctantly, "but I might have to leave early because . . . well, you know."

Rocky thought he saw a look of anger cross Bobby's face. But it was so fleeting, he wasn't sure. Then Bobby smiled and nodded. "Well, sure! You got to learn my position, right? See you later, Rock Star!"

Bobby pushed off the bench onto his crutches and made his way slowly and painstakingly across the turf to the locker room. Rocky rubbed his eyes to ward off the headache he felt coming on and then reached for his helmet.

"Schoolwork, chores, homework, football, chocolate bars, *more* football — and now campaign manager?" Rocky muttered to himself. "How am I ever going to do it all?"

**11**

**R**ocky was always tired after football practice; after his extralong session Monday afternoon, he was doubly so. He knew he should try to sell some chocolate bars after dinner that night, but he just didn't have the energy or the interest. Instead, he did his homework, watched some television, read a chapter in a science fiction novel, and then went to bed.

Tuesday morning, he ate his usual breakfast of waffles and orange juice. His mother frowned at the grungy clothes he was wearing until he told her about the walking field trip to do rock collecting. He stashed a big plastic bag in his backpack and went to school.

Mrs. Ryan's room was filled with excited chatter. It wasn't every day the class got to go on a field trip — and even though this one was just a short walk to the park, it was still better than sitting at a desk reading from a textbook.

Mrs. Ryan called for attention and everyone quieted down immediately. "I'll be breaking you into pairs," she said, "and giving each pair a rock hammer and two sets of safety glasses. The glasses belong to the school; the hammers are on loan to us for the week from the local science museum. Please treat all with care. And don't leave them behind because other classes will need to use them throughout the remainder of the week."

She read off pairs of names. Rocky and Bobby were together. She handed the small hammer to Bobby, who slipped it into his backpack.

"You can put your rock bag in there too if you want," Bobby told Rocky.

Rocky grinned. "I'll take you up on that offer — after my bag is full!"

The walk to the park took ten minutes. Rocky lagged behind with Bobby, who grunted as he moved on his crutches. Mrs. Ryan led them to the bottom of a cliff that was studded with rocks and jagged outcroppings. She instructed the students to put on their safety glasses and then demonstrated the proper technique for extracting samples from the cliff face.

"Small taps, not large whacks," she said as she knocked a walnut-size chunk free.

The students spread out across the width of the cliff. There were some loose boulders on the ground that worked well as stepping-stones to reach rocks higher up. Soon the air was filled with the sounds of metal hammer-heads tapping against stone. Every so often, someone would find a particularly interesting specimen. Then Mrs. Ryan would gather the whole class together and explain what the specimen was.

Rocky had collected seven decent-size rocks when he saw an unusual-looking formation sticking out of the cliff. It was just out of reach, however, and there were no boulders nearby for him to climb on. He stood looking up at it in frustration.

Bobby came up alongside. When he saw what Rocky was looking at, he slid one crutch out from an arm. "Use this to knock it down," he suggested.

Rocky glanced over at Mrs. Ryan. She was busy helping another student. So he took the crutch, lifted it high, and batted it against the formation. He'd only tapped it once when, suddenly, the whole thing crumbled. He managed to scramble out of the way before being hit with the pieces.

Mrs. Ryan came running. When she was certain no one was hurt, she put her hands on her hips and frowned at Rocky. "That," she said, "was not the proper technique for extracting rocks. However" — she picked up one of the bigger chunks and turned it over in her hands — "you did dislodge some intriguing specimens."

She showed the piece to Rocky and Bobby. "See the shells embedded in there? That could indicate there was once a body of water here. Interesting, yes?"

She gave the chunk to Rocky for his collection and then called to the other students. "Class, come over and help yourselves to one of Rocky's rocks! Then it's time to go back to school."

Rocky put the rock piece into his plastic bag of other samples. Bobby grabbed his own shell-studded sample and then put on his backpack and picked up his crutches.

"Help me put my stuff in my pack, will you, Rocky?" He handed his sample bag and safety glasses to Rocky. Rocky slipped them in, along with the rock hammer, his glasses, and his bag of rocks. Then he zipped up the pack.

After hobbling back from the park, Bobby

excused himself to use the bathroom at school. When he returned to the classroom, he took the hammer and two pairs of safety glasses from his pack and added them to the others already there. Then he took out his bag of rocks, put them on his desk, and set his backpack aside.

"Psst, Bobby! Can I have my samples?" Rocky whispered.

Bobby turned a confused eye to him. "Huh?"

"My rocks! Give me my rocks!"

Bobby shook his head. "I don't have your rocks!"

Rocky grabbed Bobby's backpack then. "Yes you do! I put them right in here!" He rummaged frantically inside the pack. But it was empty. "Where'd they go?"

"I don't know what you're talking about, Rocky," Bobby said. "There was only one bag of rocks in there — and it was mine!"

"Is everything okay, boys?" Mrs. Ryan asked.

"I — I lost my samples," Rocky replied. He told her what happened. "Maybe I left my bag behind. Could I go look?"

She shook her head. "I can't let you go back there without a chaperone. You'll have to go after school."

"What if they're not there anymore?"

"Take a rock hammer and pair of safety glasses with you. That way, you can gather a second set of samples if need be."

Rocky nodded dumbly. He was completely bewildered. He knew he had put his rock samples in Bobby's backpack. So where had they gone?

Then he realized what Mrs. Ryan had said. He had to go back to the park after school — but he was supposed to meet Coach Ward and the others for extra practice at three!

*If I run to the park and find my samples right away, I can still make it to the field on time,* he figured. *But if I have to dig out*

*more samples, I'll be late for sure! I may*
*even miss the extra practice time altogether!*

There was nothing to be done about it, though. Schoolwork came first, football second.

**12**

After school, Rocky raced to the cliff. He searched frantically. There was no sign of his bag of rocks anywhere. Fortunately, there were many interesting bits of rock lying on the ground, including the seashell ones he'd dislodged earlier. He gathered several good-size samples and stuck them in his backpack. They rattled around as he ran, pell-mell, for the locker room.

But even after running at top speed he was fifteen minutes late to safety practice. Coach Ward looked pointedly at his watch but nodded with understanding when Rocky explained what had happened. "I won't be late again, I promise," he assured the coach.

"See that you aren't," Coach Ward said sternly. "You don't become a good two-way player in a week by missing practice time."

The remainder of safety practice, and the regular practice that followed, went smoothly, much to Rocky's relief.

The next school day passed without mishap too. Rocky still couldn't figure out what had happened to his original samples, but now that he had others it didn't really matter.

Midway through the geology lesson, Bobby whispered a reminder to him about the student council meeting that afternoon. Rocky whispered back that he had to be on time for practice. But Bobby reassured him that the meeting would be quick. Rocky hesitated a moment longer, and then nodded that he'd be there.

So when the final school bell rang at two thirty, Rocky gathered his books and made his way to the room where the meeting was to take place. No one else was there yet so he took a seat at one of the desks to wait.

At two thirty-five, he got up and peered into the hallway. It was completely deserted. He sat back down, wondering if he had the wrong room.

The minutes ticked by. Suddenly, he heard laughter in the hall. He jumped up and hurried to the doorway. To his relief, he saw Bobby crutching his way toward him, accompanied by some other students.

"There he is! There's my campaign manager!" Bobby cried when he spotted Rocky.

"Yeah, here I am!" Rocky replied hotly. "Where have *you* been?"

Bobby blinked. "What do you mean?"

"You told me the meeting started at two thirty! It's quarter to three!"

Bobby looked apologetic. "Did I say two thirty? Oh, man, I'm sorry, Rocky, I meant three. Well, no harm done, we're all here now." He started into the room.

Rocky stood in his path. "Bobby, I can't stay, I have to go to practice. I'm going to be late as it is!"

"Okay, okay, go then!" Bobby huffed. "I'll fill you in later."

Once more, Rocky found himself running at top speed for the football field. Unfortunately, by the time he'd suited up, he was more than ten minutes late. Lars, Liam, and Jared were already practicing.

Rocky started to explain where he'd been, but Coach Ward cut him off. "Take over for Jared," he said curtly.

The coach worked the boys hard in the remaining time before regular practice. Rocky was still a little unsure of the position, but Jared seemed to have learned a great deal. In fact, Rocky noted with some surprise, Jared seemed to be enjoying his new role on the team. When the rest of the Pythons joined them, Jared joked and roughhoused with some of the defensive players.

Then Coach Ward called him over — and

the smile on Jared's face vanished, replaced with a stony expression.

*It's not football he dislikes,* Rocky realized with a jolt, *it's Coach Ward!*

Coach Royson blew his whistle then, signaling the start of practice. Jared was told to stay with the defense, Rocky to join the offense.

"We're playing the Rangers on Saturday," the coach reminded his offense. "They have the best defense in the league. To beat them, we have to have the best offense. So we're going to work on a few trick plays today. If we can master them, I have a hunch they'll fool those Rangers."

The first trick play was the flea-flicker. It was not a new play, the coach informed them, but one that professional teams had used for many years. It called for the quarterback to dish the ball to a running back. But instead of running with the ball, the back immediately dished it back to the quarterback, who looked downfield for an eligible receiver.

"Those first two moves have to be lightning fast and right on the money," the coach warned. "And the wide receivers have to be aware of who has the ball, where the defense is, and when the pass is coming. Okay, let's give it a try!"

# 13

Coach Royson lined the offense up in I-formation, with Lars behind Jeff and Rasheed behind Lars. Rasheed was to take the handoff from Jeff and return the ball to him while Lars helped block. Isaac and Rocky were told to do an "out," that is, run straight at top speed for seven yards and then cut to the sideline for the pass.

"Let's see it!" the coach called.

The play went off like clockwork. Jeff took the snap. While Lars rushed forward to block an imaginary defender, Jeff shoveled the ball into Rasheed's hands. Then Rasheed flicked the ball right back to Jeff. Jeff found

Isaac near the right sideline. Isaac looked the ball right into his hands and cradled it against his chest.

"Nicely done!" the coach praised. "Same again, only Rasheed and Lars switch places."

This time, the flea-flicker didn't work as smoothly because Lars bobbled Jeff's hand-off. The ball bounced on the ground instead of going back to Jeff.

"Start it up again!" Coach Royson called.

Rocky had done his run and now had to hurry back to his spot. Sweat trickled down his forehead, but he didn't have time to wipe it away because the players were in motion. Lars and Jeff did a perfect one-two back-and-forth, and when Jeff threw, the ball spiraled toward Rocky, who made a clean catch and danced a few more feet before turning and jogging back to the line of scrimmage.

They practiced the play until the coach was satisfied that they all had it down cold.

Sometimes Lars took the handoff, sometimes it went to Rasheed. Isaac caught several passes, as did Rocky.

The coach then taught them a similar play he called the halfback pass. In it, Jeff would once again hand off to either Lars or Rasheed, but instead of getting the ball back, the running back would be the one to throw to either Rocky or Isaac.

Rasheed was excited about the play, but Lars looked unsure. "I don't throw that well," he admitted. But he promised to do his best.

Unfortunately, his best was a weak and wobbly arc that would have landed in the arms of a defender had there been one on the field. Lars took some good-natured ribbing, but the next time, Rasheed was the one who threw.

They worked on both trick plays for twenty minutes longer. Then Coach Royson summoned the defense and announced they were going to try out their new plays against them.

"Flea-flicker," Jeff said. "Rasheed takes the handoff."

The two sides faced each other. Rocky got into his three-point stance and looked up. His eyes landed on the safety position. He was so used to seeing Bobby's face behind the helmet there that he was momentarily confused when he saw Jared's instead.

This was Jared's first time playing in a real game situation, Rocky realized. The other two practices, the defense had remained separate from the offense. Rocky wondered if Jared was nervous.

Then Jeff was calling the signals and Rocky had no more time to wonder. The ball was snapped and he took off. As he ran he imagined the ball moving from Jeff to Rasheed and back. When he guessed the ball was back with Jeff, he cut to the sideline and looked for the pass.

He hadn't gone very far when Jackson, the Pythons cornerback, raced forward to cover him. Rocky knew he was supposed to head out, but instead, he stopped short and cut inward. Jackson's momentum carried him a few steps past Rocky. Rocky, meanwhile, sped forward again, looking over his shoulder for the short pass.

It came hard, a bullet drilled right into his stomach. But that pass wasn't anywhere near as hard as the tackle he got moments later.

*Wham!* Whoever hit him did so solidly. They landed together on the turf, with Rocky on the bottom.

"Gotcha!" the defender gloated as he got to his feet.

"Jared?" Rocky had thought it was Jackson who nailed him to the ground. He stared in surprise before accepting a hand up from Jared. "*You* tackled me?"

"Don't look so amazed," Jared said. "I used to play defense in soccer, you know."

Rocky rubbed his leg, imagining the bruise that would be there tomorrow morning. "Since when do soccer players know how to flatten a guy?"

Jared gave a short laugh. "Let's just say I have some aggression to work out!"

"Sure," Rocky replied. "But how about you save it for a real game? Sheesh!"

The boys exchanged grins and then returned to their positions. The Pythons ran the trick plays over and over. While there were technically only two of them, the plays had several options each. The flea-flicker alone could start with a Jeff-Lars-Jeff or Jeff-Rasheed-Jeff combo. After that, the pass could go to either Rocky or Isaac — or even their tight end, Rocky realized, when Jeff chose to fire the ball to him after seeing that both Rocky and Isaac were covered.

Yes, Rocky was sure the trick plays would help them to victory over the Rangers. Of course, they hadn't been tested in a real game situation yet. That would happen on Saturday morning.

**14**

**R**ocky was beat after Wednesday's practice. All he wanted to do was head home, have a shower and some dinner, get his homework done, and go to bed. But when he came in the door, the phone was ringing. He hurried to answer it.

"Rocky, glad I caught you!" It was Bobby. "You're off the hook for helping me with student council."

Rocky sank down in a chair in relief. "That's gre —"

"Off the hook for thinking up a slogan, I mean," Bobby interrupted. "I already thought of one. Listen to this."

He cleared his throat and in a politician-type voice said, *"Vote for Bobby Richards. He may have only one good leg, but he'll stand firm and fight for what you want!* What do you think?" he added in his normal voice.

"Um, it's fine, I guess."

"Glad you like it because I've already printed it up on a stack of handbills. I need you to help me put them up in the hallways after school tomorrow, okay?"

Rocky closed his eyes. "Yeah, okay. But Bobby, I cannot be late for practice again. No matter what, I am leaving by two forty-five! Got it?"

"No sweat. I only have a hundred papers, it shouldn't take that long. By the way, how are the candy sales going?"

Rocky almost groaned aloud. He'd totally forgotten about the football fund-raiser! There was only a little more than two weeks remaining; if he didn't sell those chocolate bars soon, he'd wind up paying for them all himself. And with all he had to do these days, how was he supposed to earn thirty dollars?

"I'll get to it, Bobby, I promise," he said.

"Great. Because now that I've got this whole campaign thing, there's no way I could do that too. See you tomorrow, Rocky!"

Rocky called his grandparents right after he hung up and told them of his plight. They promised to buy some of the bars and to ask their friends to buy some too. They lived in the local retirement community, so Rocky arranged to come over later to deliver the candy. Then he went downstairs for dinner.

It was eight thirty before Rocky returned home from his grandparents' place. He'd sold eleven bars, but it had been slow going; everyone who bought the chocolate, including his grandparents, had a story to tell about when they were in school, or when they played football, or when they had to raise money for something. He'd listened as politely as possible but had been very happy to leave.

As he carried the remaining thirty-seven chocolate bars to his room, he tried not to think about the fact that, if he hadn't agreed to sell Bobby's candy as well as his own, he'd almost be done with the fund-raiser now. Instead, he turned his attention to his homework.

By nine o'clock, he'd finished his spelling and arithmetic. He opened his science text-book to the assigned chapter on geology. As he read, his eyelids grew heavy. His chin slowly sank to his chest. He jerked awake and shook his head to clear it.

But it was no use. He was so tired the words seemed to be swimming on the page. He closed the book and crawled into bed, telling himself he'd get up early and read before school. Then he clicked off his light, rolled onto his side, and fell fast asleep.

The alarm clock jangled before dawn the next morning. Rocky slammed his fist on the button to shut off the noise. Then he burrowed under the covers and fell back asleep. The next sound he heard was his mother's voice calling frantically for him to get up so he wouldn't be late for school.

*So much for reading!* he thought as he hurriedly threw on some clothes and stuffed his homework and books into his backpack. As it was, he barely had time to eat breakfast and brush his teeth.

Bobby caught up to him just as he was entering school. "Check it out!"

He showed Rocky one of the handbills he'd made. It pictured him standing on his crutches, looking stern and determined, with the slogan underneath. "I brought plenty of tape," Bobby added, holding up a thick roll of gray duct tape, "so we can cover this whole school with these!"

"Mmm, great," Rocky said. "Just so long as I'm outta here —"

"— by two forty-five. Absolutely. Meet me

here after the final bell and we'll get it done in no time."

To Rocky's relief, Bobby was as good as his word. They started taping up the papers at two thirty, with Bobby handing Rocky the handbills and Rocky taping them to the hallway walls. At two forty-two, Rocky handed Bobby the empty roll of tape. He was turning to leave when he heard an angry yell.

"What do you boys think you're doing?!"

It was Mr. Jenkins, the assistant principal. He was staring, aghast, at the handbills.

"Who approved the wording and image on this paper?" he asked. "Anything that is displayed at school must have approval first. And where is your slip granting you permission to put these papers up? It is strictly against the rules to do so without written permission."

Rocky looked at Bobby, waiting for him to produce the permission forms. Bobby ducked his head.

"I, uh, didn't know I needed that stuff," he said meekly.

Mr. Jenkins tore down one of the papers. "Both policies were clearly outlined in yesterday's student council meeting! You must take down every single one of these immediately! And don't just throw the papers away. This school is making every attempt to 'go green.' So separate the paper from the tape and put the sheets in the appropriate recycle bins."

He handed Bobby the handbill and stalked away.

Rocky turned to Bobby in dismay. "How could you not know? Weren't you listening during the meeting?"

"I guess I missed that part." Bobby leaned against the wall and rubbed his leg above the cast. "Man, this thing is aching all of a sudden. You'll help me take all this stuff down, won't you?"

Rocky had been on the verge of storming away. But the sight of Bobby in pain made him stop. So he swallowed his frustration, reached up, and started pulling down hand-bills.

*So much for safety practice,* he thought. *Coach Ward is going to kill me.*

**15**

**C**oach Ward didn't kill him, of course, but he did chew him out good and long.

Fortunately, Rocky made it to safety practice on time on Friday. But that night, he had trouble falling asleep because he was worried about the next day's game. When he did finally drift off, his dreams were troubled.

Rocky awoke close to dawn and couldn't get back to sleep. So he dressed, left a note for his parents saying he'd gone for a walk, and stepped out into the gray-blue light of early morning.

He walked aimlessly and wound up near

the park. He was blowing clouds of breath into the air when, suddenly, he heard a sound. He looked around and saw a boy about his age. Rocky couldn't tell who it was at first. Then he saw that the boy had a soccer ball with him — and realized it was Jared.

Jared bounced the ball from knee to knee for more than a minute. When the ball finally fell to the ground, he began to dribble. Rocky stared in admiration as Jared's feet flew over the dewy grass, guiding the ball with sure taps.

Then Jared stopped short and booted the ball with a solid kick. He punched the air with his fist as if celebrating a goal and then raced to retrieve the ball. When he turned, he saw Rocky and froze.

Rocky hurried over to him. "Man, you really know how to handle that ball!"

Jared relaxed. "Thanks. My dad used to work with me on that stuff."

"Used to?" The second the words were

out, Rocky wished he could pull them back. It wasn't any of his business why Jared's dad had stopped playing soccer with him.

Jared dropped the ball and nudged it with his toe. "My mom and dad got divorced two years ago and my dad moved away. I hardly ever see him now. Instead, I'm stuck with my stepdad." He practically spat out that last word.

"Oh. You don't like him much, huh?"

"What's to like?" Jared eyed Rocky. "Would you want him as your stepfather?"

Rocky blinked. "How should I know? I don't even know who he is."

Jared gave the soccer ball another mighty kick. "Yeah, you do. You just don't know it. No one is supposed to know."

Rocky was totally bewildered by now. "What is it that no one is supposed to know?"

"That Coach Ward is my stepfather."

Rocky's jaw dropped. "Get out of town!"

Jared gave a short laugh. "Yeah, half of the

time I can't believe it either. But it's true. He married my mom over the summer."

"Why isn't anyone supposed to know you're related?"

Jared flared up at that. "We're *not* related!"

Then he took a deep breath and calmed down. "He's worried the other Pythons will think he's playing favorites if anyone found out. But that's such a joke! I didn't even want to be on his stupid team! No offense to the Pythons," he added hurriedly.

"Then why the heck did you join?" Rocky asked.

"My mother thought it would be a good way for Coach Ward and me to get to know each other better." Jared kicked at the grass. "But all it's done is make my soccer friends mad. See, they don't know about Coach Ward either. They think I ditched them to play football. Now they won't even talk to me." He gave Rocky a sidelong glance. "And until this week, the football guys wouldn't talk to me either."

Rocky shifted uncomfortably. "Sorry about that," he mumbled at last. "So why didn't you just tell your mom you wanted to stick with soccer?"

Jared lifted a shoulder. "She laid down a major guilt trip on me. About how I wasn't even trying to get along with the coach and how I was making it so difficult for us to be a happy family, blah blah blah. After that, it was hard to say no." He sighed. "Anyone ever guilt trip you into doing something you didn't really want to do?"

"Me? Nah," Rocky replied. "So, is that why you agreed to play safety too? To make your mom happy?"

Jared snorted. "No, I agreed to play safety because I was bored out of my skull sitting on the bench waiting to kick the dumb football! Now at least I'll get into the game more."

Rocky laughed. "A lot more, probably. You know, for someone who hasn't been playing football for long, you're pretty good at it. Better than me at safety, anyway."

Jared gave him a quick look. "You'd be good too if you ever made it to practice on time!"

"Don't remind me," Rocky said, shaking his head. "I can still hear Coach Ward yelling at me."

"Why have you been late so much, anyway?" Jared asked.

"Let's see." Rocky ticked off the reasons on his fingers. "Thursday, I had to help Bobby take down about a hundred handbills we weren't supposed to have put up in the first place. The day before that, I sat in an empty room waiting for Bobby and other student council candidates to show up for a meeting that Bobby had told me started at two thirty, but really started at three. And Tuesday, I had to go collect a second bunch of rock samples because the first batch disappeared — even though I'm sure I put them in Bobby's backpack!" He sighed. "And on top of all that, I still haven't sold hardly any of my chocolate bars, although I did manage to unload Bobby's for him."

He looked up then to see Jared staring at him curiously. "What?"

"Nothing. It's just . . . well, does Bobby always have you doing so much stuff for him?"

# 16

Rocky stared back at Jared. Then he looked away. "I guess I have been doing a lot of stuff for Bobby lately," he mumbled. "But only because I broke his leg."

"Huh. When you say it like that, it sounds like you meant to break it."

"Of course I didn't!" Rocky protested. "It was an accident. But it was still my fault. If I hadn't tackled him, he wouldn't have hit the bench and broken his leg."

Jared considered this for a long moment. "Okay, sure," he said finally, "but go back one step more. *Why* did you tackle him?"

"He took my music player even though I'd

asked him to leave it alone. And he was making fun of me in front of you guys."

"So if he hadn't done those things, you wouldn't have tackled him, and —"

"— and his leg wouldn't be broken!" Rocky widened his eyes with understanding then. "Man, I never looked at it that way before! I guess it really wasn't *all* my fault, was it?"

"It was just a freak accident," Jared agreed. "And the floor was wet, which it shouldn't have been. You shouldn't blame yourself — and Bobby shouldn't blame you either. *And* he shouldn't make you feel guilty for it."

"Bobby isn't making me . . ."

Rocky's protest died on his lips because, suddenly, he wondered if Jared was right. He remembered too how angry Bobby had been when he thought Vincent was taking over his position and when he found out Jared was to learn it. He also remembered how relieved he'd been that Bobby hadn't been angry with him too.

But what if he had been angry? What if he was *still* angry? Would he take out his anger on Rocky by guilt-tripping him into doing him favors — favors that would keep him from the practice field?

Rocky turned to Jared then and told him of his suspicions. As he did, he felt his temper start to rise. Bobby was supposed to be his best friend!

Jared nodded slowly when Rocky was done. "There's only one way to know for sure if you're right. Ask him."

Rocky stuck his hands in his pockets and tightened them into fists. "Oh, I'm going to ask him, all right. And I'm going to tell him a thing or two too!"

Rocky started to storm out of the park.

"Hold up, Rocky!" Jared cried. "You and Bobby have been friends for a long time. So *talk* to him, don't *yell* at him. Find out why he's been acting the way he has. Then try to work it out between you."

Rocky rounded on him. "Is that what you

101

did with your mom and Coach Ward?" he asked angrily. He regretted his words the instant they were out of his mouth. Jared was only trying to help him, after all.

But Jared took it in stride. "No, I didn't. I yelled and screamed and shouted. And look where it got me — nowhere!"

Rocky's anger waned. "Okay. I'll talk and I'll listen. But he better have some darned good reasons for treating me the way he has!"

Rocky and Jared parted company then. Rocky took the long way home, past Bobby's house. But when he knocked, no one answered.

"I'll find him at the game," he decided as he walked to his own house.

"There you are!" his father said when Rocky came into the kitchen. "I was about to send out a search party. You'd better get some breakfast. We have to leave for your game in half an hour."

**17**

**T**wo bowls of cereal and a glass of orange juice later, Rocky and his parents were on their way to the football field. It was a glorious morning for a game, sunny but not too bright, with a cool breeze wafting through the red-and-gold leaves of the trees.

Rocky barely noticed the weather, however. He was too busy looking for Bobby. He didn't see him. Then it was time for warmups and the game started soon after.

The Rangers had won the toss so the Pythons were kicking off. As Jared jogged onto the field, someone called out, "Send it into the stratosphere!"

Jared raised his hand in acknowledgment. Then he readied himself for the kick.

*Fweet!* The official blew his whistle. Jared ran forward and booted the ball high into the sky.

The Rangers got under it and made the catch at their own forty-three-yard line. Their blockers cleared a path but the Pythons biggest lineman, Alan Dobbs, broke through and flattened the ball carrier with a dead-on tackle.

There was a shuffle as players from both special teams left the field to make way for the incoming offense and defense. Jared, who was starting out in the safety spot, remained on the field. He danced from foot to foot as if he was nervous.

He had every reason to be. Coach Royson had warned the Pythons that the Rangers were a top-notch defensive squad. It turned out their offense was nearly as strong. Their quarterback stood inches taller than most of the other players. He also had a rocket of a throw. With his extra height, he was able to send his powerful passes over the outstretched hands of most of the Pythons linemen and linebackers. That left the cornerbacks and the safeties to stop the play.

Unfortunately, the Pythons secondary didn't do that, not at first, anyway. The Rangers quickly marched down the gridiron with a series of short, sharp passes. Three of the passes were caught by the receiver Jared was supposed to be covering.

Rocky felt bad for him. Jared had seemed to be playing so well — had told Rocky he was actually enjoying football now that he was playing safety. But today, he looked like the football newbie he really was. Rocky wondered how much longer Coach Ward would keep his stepson in the game.

Not much longer, it turned out. "Rocky! Sub in for Jared!" the coach called.

Rocky stuck in his mouth guard and headed out onto the field. Jared gave a curt nod when Rocky approached.

"Jared! Come here a minute," Coach Ward called then.

For a split second, Rocky thought Jared would steer clear of his stepfather. But after a brief hesitation, Jared joined him at the sidelines. The two were in deep conversation when Rocky got into his stance.

"Shut 'em down, shut 'em down," he muttered to himself. "Quick feet, one eye on the ball, one eye on the receivers. Here we go!"

The Rangers quarterback took the snap and faded back. He shoved the ball into the arms of one of his running backs.

Or did he?

Rocky recognized the fake in the same instant he saw the Rangers tight end barrel through the defense and look back for the pass.

*Oh, no you don't!* Rocky put on a burst of speed. The quarterback threw. Rocky reached the tight end just before the ball. He thrust out his hand to slap down the pass.

*Thwack!* To his horror, his fingers didn't hit the ball — they hit the tight end's face mask and got caught in the grill!

A whistle shrieked. A yellow flag sailed through the air next to him. All play stopped instantly.

"Face mask!" the official called. "Five-yard penalty against the defense!"

There was a collective groan and loud booing from the stands. Rocky wished he could tell the official that he hadn't meant to grab the mask. But he knew it would be useless to argue the call. So he just trotted with the rest of his team to the new line of scrimmage.

# 18

Rocky's penalty put the Rangers in good scoring position. They took full advantage of it too with an unexpected running play that found the tight end plunging over the end zone.

*Fweet!* Touchdown!

Rocky lined up for the extra-point attempt. The Rangers went for two — and got them with yet another short pass from their star quarterback.

Rocky jogged off the field feeling completely miserable, knowing he was responsible for his team's eight-point deficit. He vowed to turn things around when he took to the gridiron again on offense. In the meantime, he grabbed a cup of water and walked over to where Jared stood watching the return team set up for the Rangers kickoff.

"I saw you talking with Coach Ward," Rocky said in a low voice. "That go okay?"

Jared nodded and took a drink from his own cup. "I talked to him before the game too," he confided. "Him and my mom. I laid it all out for them — about how I'd felt guilt-tripped into playing football, how my soccer buddies were ignoring me, all that stuff."

"Wow. That took guts. Did they listen to what you were saying?"

"For the most part, they did. Probably because this time, I wasn't yelling. I told the coach that I was beginning to like football too, but that I liked soccer better."

"What did he say?"

Jared grinned. "He said he heard about a new indoor soccer league that plays during the winter and that I should definitely sign up for a team! That's when I told him he should coach it!" His grin faded then. "Did you talk to Bobby yet?"

Rocky shook his head. "He wasn't home. And I haven't seen him here. Have you?"

"Nope." There was a loud cheer from the stands then. The Pythons had returned the ball for more than thirty yards.

Jared nudged him. "Looks like you're up, cowboy. Go get 'em!"

Rocky ran onto the field and joined the huddle. Jeff, usually calm, cool, and collected, seemed excited. "Coach wants us to do the flea-flicker right away. Rasheed takes the handoff. Isaac, Rocky, you guys slant out and cut back in. Ready? Break!"

Jeff's excitement was contagious. Rocky sprinted to his spot and got into his stance with his heart in his mouth.

*Gonna make it happen!* he told himself.

Jeff barked out the signals. Joe snapped the ball. Lars charged forward to help block while Jeff danced back and handed the ball to Rasheed.

The Rangers defense swarmed the running back, clearly expecting him to rush with the ball. But before they could reach him, Rasheed dished the ball back to Jeff.

Rocky, meanwhile, was doing everything he could to get clear of his defender. He cut out, slanted in, ran straight, and spun back.

Now the Rangers turned toward the Pythons quarterback. Their defensive tackle was only steps away when Jeff launched a long bomb in Rocky's direction.

Rocky did a mental fast-forward to picture where the ball would come down. He dashed to that spot at top speed. The cornerback shadowed him all the way. But at the last moment, Rocky threw himself horizontally through the air. Arms outstretched, he reached for the ball — and snared it at the Rangers thirty-six a split second before his chest hit the dirt!

The officials signaled that the pass was

complete and that the Pythons had made first down. The crowd roared. Rocky's teammates thumped his shoulder pads and helmet. Then they huddled up to hear the next play. This time, it was a simple run up the middle by Lars.

"Punch me a wide enough hole," Lars growled, "and I'll charge right on through it!"

He was as good as his word — better even, for after blasting though the opening he strong-armed one tackle out of the way and dove beneath another for extra ground. In all, the play gained them six yards.

Second down and four to go. Jeff called for a bootleg, with a fake to Rasheed. "Rocky, Isaac, go short this time. We just need four."

They didn't get the four, however, because the Rangers blitzed and dropped Jeff for a loss of three.

Third down and seven. Jeff no longer looked excited; he looked grim. "They'll be looking for the long bomb again," he said. "And that's what we'll do — but the pass won't come from me. Rasheed, you feel up to throwing?"

"Bring it on," Rasheed replied.

"I'll take that as a yes. Halfback pass. Receivers, get into that end zone and give him a target. Break!"

**19**

Adrenaline rushed through Rocky's veins as he got into his stance. His leg muscles tightened with anticipation. *Steady, steady,* he said to himself as Jeff called the play, *a-a-and . . . NOW!*

At the snap, Rocky shot forward like an arrow from a bow. Jeff flicked the ball to Rasheed. Rocky darted into the end zone and hooked out toward the flags. Rasheed pump-faked the ball in a perfect imitation of Jeff.

When he threw, however, the ball wobbled instead of spiraled. But the throw had height and distance and when the ball came down it landed smack in Isaac's waiting hands and stuck there. Touchdown!

"Beautiful!" Rocky crowed. He didn't care that he hadn't made the catch. He was just happy the Pythons had scored. So were his teammates. On the extra-point attempt, they rode their momentum into the end zone for two more on the scoreboard. The game was now tied 8 to 8.

Rocky ran off the field, high-fiving Jared who was running on for the kickoff. The Rangers returned it for twenty yards and the Pythons defense took to the field. As before, Jared stayed in at safety.

Rocky went to the cooler to fill his bottle with water.

"So, the coach is playing the newbie in my spot, huh?" Rocky looked up to see Bobby crutching his way toward the bench. "What's the matter, Rock Star, aren't you good enough to play it?"

Rocky's temper flared then. "Maybe I

would be good enough," he spat, "if you'd let me get to practice on time this week!"

Bobby jerked back as if Rocky had taken a swing at him. Suddenly off balance, he started to fall. Rocky caught him by the arm to steady him and then let go.

Bobby sank down on the bench, rubbed his arm, and gave Rocky an injured look. "My leg, ow, my arm, I think you —"

Rocky cut him off. "Save it, Bobby. I'm through letting you make me feel guilty. In fact, maybe it's your turn to feel guilty — guilty for keeping me from learning your position!"

Bobby blinked. "What're you talking about? I didn't —"

"The chocolate bars? The student council stuff? And what about my rock collection, Bobby? Did you get rid of my bag of rocks just so I'd be late to practice that day too?"

Rocky hadn't really believed Bobby had done anything with his rock collection. But then he saw a look of shame cross Bobby's face — and he knew he'd hit on the truth. All the anger went out of him then, replaced instead with hurt. He slumped down on the bench.

"Geez, Bobby, I thought you were my friend."

"I am." Bobby's voice was a mere whisper, barely audible over the shouts of the crowd.

"Then . . . why?"

"I don't know. I guess I was sore at you."

"For breaking your leg? It was an accident!"

"An accident that wouldn't have happened if you'd just let me use your music player!" Bobby said.

"An accident that wouldn't have happened if you hadn't taken it after I asked you not to!" Rocky retorted.

They fell silent. Then Bobby spoke again.

"I didn't mean to," he said. "To take advantage of you, I mean. It's just . . . when you told me you were taking over my position, it was like you stabbed me in the back. I love playing football and I was going to have a great season, I know I was! Then this" — he thumped his cast angrily — "ended it all. I — it wasn't fair, that's all."

Rocky drew a deep breath and let it out slowly. "What wasn't fair was the way you treated me. But I guess I'm partly to blame. You're one of my best friends. I should have known you were upset." He gave a half smile. "And I really should have said no to some of the things you were asking me to do!"

A smile crept over Bobby's face too. "I should have let you know I was mad. If I had, we would have gotten this out of the way a week ago — and I wouldn't be stuck running for student council!" He made a disgusted face.

Rocky laughed. "And I wouldn't have been stuck selling your chocolate bars!"

Bobby had the decency to look ashamed at that. "Say, Rocky, how about I sell the rest of them, huh?" He stuck out his hand then. "Friends again?"

Rocky shook it. "Absolutely."

"Awesome." There was a loud shout from the field. Bobby craned his neck around to try to see what was happening. "Say, Rock Star, I just have one last favor to ask . . ."

Rocky groaned. "*Now* what?"

"Move your caboose so I can swing my leg — my poor, poor, broken leg — onto the bench and watch the rest of the game!"

And that, Rocky found, was one favor he didn't mind doing.

# MATT CHRISTOPHER

THE #1
SPORTS SERIES
FOR KIDS

®

## Read them all!

- Baseball Flyhawk
- Baseball Pals
- Baseball Turnaround
- The Basket Counts
- Body Check
- Catch That Pass!
- Catcher with a Glass Arm
- Catching Waves
- Center Court Sting
- Centerfield Ballhawk
- Challenge at Second Base
- The Comeback Challenge
- Comeback of the Home Run Kid
- Cool as Ice
- The Diamond Champs
- Dirt Bike Racer

- Dirt Bike Runaway
- Dive Right In
- Double Play at Short
- Face-Off
- Fairway Phenom
- Football Double Threat
- Football Fugitive
- Football Nightmare
- The Fox Steals Home
- Goalkeeper in Charge
- The Great Quarterback Switch
- Halfback Attack*
- The Hockey Machine
- Ice Magic
- Johnny Long Legs
- The Kid Who Only Hit Homers

*Previously published as Crackerjack Halfback

Lacrosse Face-Off

Lacrosse Firestorm

Line Drive to Short**

Long-Arm Quarterback

Long Shot for Paul

Look Who's Playing First Base

Miracle at the Plate

Mountain Bike Mania

Nothin' But Net

Penalty Shot

The Reluctant Pitcher

Return of the Home Run Kid

Run For It

Shoot for the Hoop

Shortstop from Tokyo

Skateboard Renegade

Skateboard Tough

Slam Dunk

Snowboard Champ

Snowboard Maverick

Snowboard Showdown

Soccer Duel

Soccer Halfback

Soccer Hero

Soccer Scoop

Stealing Home

The Submarine Pitch

The Team That Couldn't Lose

Tennis Ace

Tight End

Top Wing

Touchdown for Tommy

Tough to Tackle

Wingman on Ice

The Year Mom Won the Pennant

All available in paperback from Little, Brown and Company

**Previously published as Pressure Play

# Matt Christopher®

| | |
|---|---|
| Muhammad Ali | Randy Johnson |
| Lance Armstrong | Michael Jordan |
| Kobe Bryant | Peyton and Eli Manning |
| Jennifer Capriati | Yao Ming |
| Dale Earnhardt Sr. | Shaquille O'Neal |
| Jeff Gordon | Jackie Robinson |
| Ken Griffey Jr. | Alex Rodriguez |
| Mia Hamm | Babe Ruth |
| Tony Hawk | Curt Schilling |
| Ichiro | Sammy Sosa |
| LeBron James | Tiger Woods |
| Derek Jeter | |